THE DECKCHAIR DETECTIVES

Martin Oliver

Illustrated by Paddy Mounter

Designed by Paul Greenleaf

Series Editor: Gaby Waters

Assistant Editor: Rachael Robinson

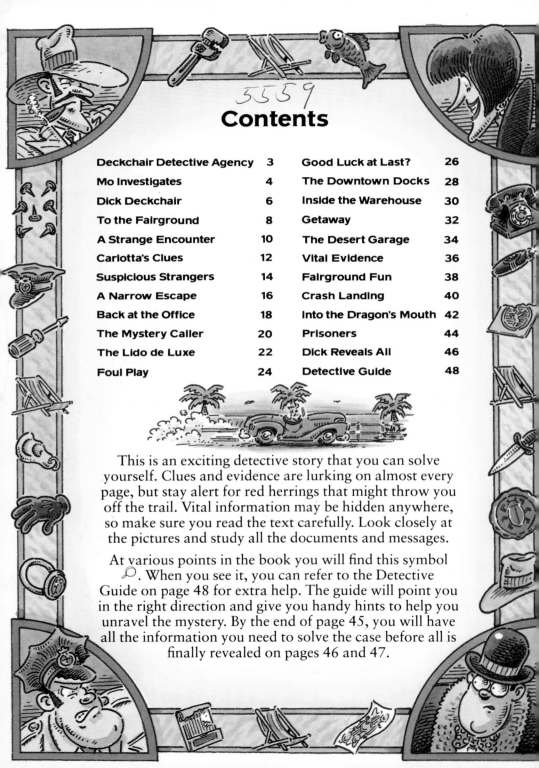

Contents

This is an exciting detective story that you can solve yourself. Clues and evidence are lurking on almost every page, but stay alert for red herrings that might throw you off the trail. Vital information may be hidden anywhere, so make sure you read the text carefully. Look closely at the pictures and study all the documents and messages.

At various points in the book you will find this symbol ⌕. When you see it, you can refer to the Detective Guide on page 48 for extra help. The guide will point you in the right direction and give you handy hints to help you unravel the mystery. By the end of page 45, you will have all the information you need to solve the case before all is finally revealed on pages 46 and 47.

Deckchair Detective Agency

DECKCHAIR DETECTIVE AGENCY.

Seeks experienced detective.

Fourth Floor, Seaview Mansions,
Palm Tree Plaza.
Telephone #032465.

Mo Jackson gulped and tried to control her jangling nerves as the
ancient elevator clunked to a halt on the fourth floor of a grimy
apartment building. She pushed the cage across and stepped out onto a
dusty landing. Mo looked to her left and spotted the words 'Deckchair
Detective Agency' on a glass door.

"Well, this is it. My big chance to become a detective," Mo thought as
she glanced down to check the advertisement she had ripped out of a
newspaper. "I may not have much experience, but at least I look the part
in my supersleuth gear."

Mo stepped over to the door. She pushed her coat collar up, then tilted
the brim of her hat down. Hoping that she looked more confident than
she felt, Mo knocked on the door.

Mo Investigates

The door slowly creaked open a few inches. Mo hesitated for a second, waiting for someone to appear, but no one did. She shrugged her shoulders and stepped cautiously into the Deckchair Detective Agency. Her eyes opened wide with surprise.

The room was in chaos. Mo cast her private eye's eye over the mess. Her brain raced as she took in the overturned chair, the papers spilling out of drawers and the objects scattered across the floor. It looked as if the office had been ransacked.

"Hello, is anyone there?" she asked, but there was no reply. Sweat trickled down her face as a wave of warm, stale air wafted towards her. Overhead a ceiling fan whirred wearily, disturbing the top layer of dust and making the musty old papers flutter lazily. It was all very strange. Mo decided to investigate.

CREAK. A floorboard groaned as Mo walked up to the window. She stopped beside a filing cabinet. A large, hairy fly was buzzing angrily at the dirty pane of glass. Light filtered into the room through the broken slats of a grubby blind.

Ignoring a twinge of guilt, Mo began to flick through some of the yellowing papers inside the top drawer. She looked at the date on them and frowned – they were all ten years old or more. The contents of a lunch box didn't look much younger either. But just then, out of the corner of her eye, she spotted something that had been freshly made.

A trail of footprints in the dust led towards the back door. Who had made them? Was it an intruder? Was it the person who had ransacked the office? Mo had to find out.

She tiptoed up to the door and stopped in her tracks as she heard a strange sound coming from outside. What was it? Human without a doubt. There it was again, and again. It sounded like someone struggling for air. What was going on?

"This is it," Mo thought suddenly. "At last, a chance to prove myself as a private eye." In her mind she could see the headlines on tomorrow's front pages – *Detective unravels mystery of ransacked office.*

But what if there was a dangerous criminal outside? Mo gulped, then steeled herself for action. With a single bound she kicked open the door. "Come out with your hands up," she shouted. "We've got the place surrounded."

Dick Deckchair

A startled yell answered Mo's shout. It was followed by a crash and an ominous ripping sound. Mo stepped out onto a metal fire escape. She blinked her eyes in the bright sunlight and then focused on a bewildered looking figure who was staring back at her from underneath a broken deckchair.

Mo's shoulders slumped. Suddenly her coat felt much too big and far too hot. Her hat began to itch. She had been imagining things again. The person entangled in the deckchair didn't look much like a dangerous criminal and there was probably a perfectly normal explanation for the chaotic mess in the office.

A loud 'ouch' brought her attention back to the figure who was still trying to untangle himself from the remains of the deckchair. Mo helped him to his feet, then she introduced herself.

"Hello, I'm Mo Jackson. I'm looking for the Deckchair Detective Agency."

"You found it. I AM the agency. My name's Dick Deckchair."

"You don't look much like a detective."

"Of course I don't. If I did, everyone would know I was one. What do you want?"

"Er, I came about the job."

"That explains the fancy dress."

6

"I've just taken over the old family firm," Dick explained. "It's been a bit neglected but now I'm in charge, business is bound to boom. I'm determined to make it work. That's why I want an experienced detective to join me as a partner. What cases have you worked on?"

Mo admitted that she hadn't actually been involved in any cases yet. "But I know that I've got what it takes to be a detective," she said confidently. "If only I can have a chance."

"I don't know," Dick answered. "I'm a natural, you see. Just now I was taking a breather from office paperwork and polishing up my detecting techniques. You'd be amazed at the cases I've solved from my deckchair. The key to being a top 'tec is observation. You must always keep your eyes peeled and be on the alert for anything unusual."

"I agree, definitely," Mo replied. "Take that fire at the fairground for example. That's fairly unusual."

To the Fairground

Dick spun around. "Fire ...?" he spluttered, staring at the billowing plume of smoke in the distance. Then he recovered. "Well done," he blustered. "You've passed the first test. I was wondering when you'd spot that little spark."

Just then there was a loud knock at the office door. Dick looked startled. Then he grasped Mo's hand and gave it a firm shake.

"Welcome to the agency," he said. "Your first job is to answer the door." And with that, he shot off down the fire escape.

By now, Mo could hear heavy banging on the door. She didn't like the sound of it. "Hey," she shouted, racing after him. "Wait for me. What's the rush?"

"It's Great Aunt Bertha," he shouted over his shoulder as he shot off down the fire escape. "I'd recognize that knock anywhere..."

Dick was already behind the wheel of a battered jalopy when Mo jumped off the fire escape. He hit the accelerator. Mo clung on by her fingertips. She scrambled into the front seat then spotted a book on the floor. "How to be a good detective," Mo read aloud. "With pictures."

"OK, so neither of us are hot-shot detectives," Dick admitted. "But together we might make a good team. What do you say?"

"Maybe," said Mo. "First of all, let's check out that fire."

Minutes later the car bumped over rough wasteland and pulled up outside the fair. Dick and Mo got out and dashed up to the entrance. A plume of black smoke still hung in the air, but they couldn't see any flames. Maybe they were too late and had missed all the action.

"Come on," Mo said, ignoring the large sign by the entrance. "Let's go in and find out what's been going on."

They had just squeezed through the rusty turnstile when a dark shadow fell across their path. Dick looked up at a huge security guard blocking their way.

"Can't you read?" the guard snapped. "We're closed. Now scram."

Get out of here . . . and fast.

Mo and Dick looked at each other. They weren't going to be pushed around by this bully. Then Dick had an idea. He fished into his pocket and pulled out his ID card. This should impress him, Dick thought.

It didn't. Dick and Mo gulped as heavy hands gripped their collars and their feet left the ground. Dick started to complain but his squeaky protests fell on deaf ears and he was lifted higher, legs kicking helpessly.

"I don't care if you're a deckchair detective or a defective deckchair," the guard snarled. "I've got my orders. You're not supposed to be here, and don't even think of coming back."

Dick and Mo tried to wriggle free of the iron grip, but the guard wouldn't let go. He was hauling the dangling detectives towards the exit when a throaty voice suddenly stopped him. "OK Tom. Put them down. I'll talk to them in my office."

A Strange Encounter

Mo looked around as her feet hit the floor. There was no sign of whoever had given the order, but the security guard was certainly obeying it. He pushed Dick and Mo down a narrow alley between The World of Wax and a shooting gallery. They stepped over power cables and ducked under steel girders then stopped at the back door of a tall building.

"This must be the office," Dick muttered. "Just keep quiet and let me handle this."

The door swung open and Dick and Mo were shoved inside. Dick's eyes opened wide at what he saw. He turned white and his legs wobbled. Mo turned to run, just as the door slammed shut. The sound of a key rattling in the lock echoed through the chamber.

"W..w..what sort of office is this?" Dick stuttered. "It's some sort of trap. We'll never get out of here." Mo shook her foot free of a mechanical arm and nearly tripped over something on the floor – it was a railway track. Her brain raced as she stared around the dingy dungeon. Suddenly it clicked. They were inside the Ghost Train.

10

Dick slowly turned less green once Mo told him what she had realized. He chuckled as he flicked the legs of a rubber spider. While he was making faces at a grinning skull, Mo spotted a newspaper lying on the blade of a plastic guillotine.

"Look at this," she said to Dick, brandishing the paper. "Both of these stories mention the fairground. It looks as though there have been other fires here before."

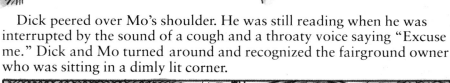

A DAUGHTER'S DESPERATE APPEAL

Tearful Viola Dodgem, daughter of missing ex-fairground owner, David Dodgem, appealed to the public for information that might lead to his whereabouts.

"He has been very nervous recently. He said he had discovered something important through an old fairground acquaintance."

FAIRGROUND FIRES

Since purchasing the city fairground one year ago, Carlotta Bottle has been dogged by bad luck. Although nobody has been hurt, two fires in last month have drastically reduced the numb of visitors. Now Carlotta has spoken to THE GLOBE to assure customers that the fair is safe.

Dick peered over Mo's shoulder. He was still reading when he was interrupted by the sound of a cough and a throaty voice saying "Excuse me." Dick and Mo turned around and recognized the fairground owner who was sitting in a dimly lit corner.

"I hope my office didn't alarm you," said Carlotta Bottle, smiling as Dick shook his head decisively. "I am looking for a detective and you two might just be able to help me. I need you to find the person who is starting the fires at my fairground."

Carlotta's Clues

Mo's brain raced. This was it – their big chance! "We'd be delighted to help," she replied. "Efficiency, speed and success. That's our motto, isn't it Dick?"

"Er, yes definitely," Dick replied. "But are you sure the fires were started deliberately? Do you have any idea who might be behind them?"

"The culprit is David Dodgem – I'm sure of that," Carlotta answered. "But I don't know why he is doing it, or where he is hiding."

Carlotta emptied out a box file. "That's Dodgem," she said, pointing to two photos of a suspicious-looking character. "I wrote out a list of rides and took the other photos at the scene of the crime where I found the incriminating evidence – one of Dodgem's gloves and a butt of his usual cigar brand. Go ahead, you can pick them up."

While Dick and Mo examined the evidence, Carlotta stood up and yanked a piece of cord. A blind shot up revealing a window overlooking the fair.

"Dodgem used to own the fair until I took over a year ago," Carlotta breathed. "I know he's out there. He may still have accomplices working here."

"I know there's not much to go on, but you are my only hope. When you find him, let me know at once. No one else at the fair must know what you are doing..."

Just then Mo's ears pricked up as she heard a faint sound outside. She dashed over to the door and yanked it open. A familiar figure fell into the room. "Oh... hello Carlotta," the security guard stammered. "I was um... checking that these two weren't causing any trouble."

"Thanks for your concern Tom," Carlotta answered coldly. "But Dick and Mo are old friends of mine. What's the news on the latest fire?"

"It's bad, I'm afraid," Tom replied, shaking his head. "The Wall of Death is badly damaged and Max, the operator, has disappeared."

Dick stood up. It was time to investigate. A Deckchair Detective might find clues at the scene of a crime where an amateur would see nothing. As he and Mo turned to leave, Carlotta scribbled on a piece of paper and pressed it into Mo's hand. "This is my number," she explained. "Contact me when you have news."

They stepped outside and set off in search of the Wall of Death. "Follow me," Dick said. "And don't forget what Carlotta said – Dodgem might still have accomplices here. Stay alert, keep your eyes and ears open."

Dick walked down past the side of the Hall of Mirrors. Mo was right beside him, when all of a sudden she stopped dead in her tracks.

Max had it coming to him. He was sticking his nose into our business. He must have found the entrance mechanism.

"Listen," she hissed pointing to a window behind her. Dick and Mo strained their ears and heard a man's voice whispering. What he was saying sounded very suspicious. Dick tiptoed up to the window and peered inside.

13

Suspicious Strangers

Max was starting to cause trouble. The boss was right. We had to get rid of him.

I reckon he was snooping for Sharkey. His mob is after us again.

Same as that interfering watchman down at the docks.

(5) Dick's eyes boggled at what he saw, then he realized he was looking at distorted reflections of three people. He couldn't see their faces clearly, but he understood what the trio were saying. They had disposed of Max, but who were they? Who was 'the boss' and who was 'Sharkey'?

Dick and Mo needed to get a closer look at the strange trio. They were creeping up to the front of the Hall of Mirrors when a strangely-clad apparition materialized in a cloud of smoke and blocked their way. "Who... who are you?" Dick asked, astonished.

"I am Clare Voyant," the figure replied. "I see danger before you. Be on your guard." As she finished speaking, the woman wrapped her cape around her and disappeared in a swirl of purple, leaving a faint smell of violets, and Dick and Mo open-mouthed with amazement.

"Come on Dick," Mo whispered, snapping herself back to attention. "I'm not letting some old phoney frighten us off the case, we've still got to get a good look at those three characters in the mirrors."

They crept inside the Hall of Mirrors, but it was empty. The strange trio had disappeared without trace, or had they? Dick spotted a scrap of paper on the floor. The message on it was strange, and so was the wax seal. What was it all about? Dick had a hunch it might be **(6)** useful in the future. He put it in his pocket and they headed for the Wall of Death.

Congratulations on carrying out your task today. You're needed for the shift tonight. Another consignment must be ready at the docks by midnight. Watch out for Sharkey and his mob.

Minutes later, Dick stared up at the smouldering remains of the ride. The air was still thick with the smell of burning wood, and ash was gently drifting down onto the scorched earth. Dick kept a safe distance from the damaged ride and bent down to check the ground for clues. Nothing. He straightened up just in time to see Mo disappear through the main doors.

"There may be some evidence inside," she shouted. "Keep an eye open while I go in and investigate."

Before Dick could stop her, Mo was gone. Dick looked around uneasily. Out of the corner of his eye he glimpsed a purple shadow, but then it was gone. A sudden gust of wind made the rickety structure groan and sway. A piece of wood clattered to the ground, followed by another, then another. Dick shouted out a desperate warning.

15

A Narrow Escape

Dick raced up to the Wall of Death but he tripped over an empty bucket and went flying, just as the structure sagged slightly to the left and collapsed with a thundering crash. Dick kept his head down. As soon as the last lethal fragment of flying debris had whistled past his ears, he staggered up and wobbled over to find Mo.

A pile of shattered planks moved, then coughed. Mo opened her eyes and sat up shakily. "I'm fine," she spluttered to Dick. "But I think we'd better get going before anyone finds us here. We're supposed to be working undercover."

Dick glanced over his shoulder. Fairground workers were heading over to what had once been the Wall of Death, and none of them looked very happy. Dick dragged Mo out of the wreckage.

"Come on, let's go" Mo panted. She leaned against Dick for support and they half-staggered, half-sprinted away. As Mo gradually recovered, they accelerated to increase the distance between themselves and the angry shouts behind. "Why did you go into that death trap?" Dick asked. as they dashed around a corner. "Don't tell me you found some important evidence in that ruin."

SMACK. Before Mo could answer she crashed straight into Tom. She lay on the floor, winded as the security guard towered over them.

"I thought I'd already told you two to scram," he hissed angrily. Then his voice softened. "It's dangerous here. If anyone else had found you, it would have been curtains. You must leave."

Tom pointed down a passageway that ran between a row of trailers and some power generators. "Head that way, take the third opening on the left and you'll find a gap in the fence. Now get out of here."

They went. Mo was first under the wire and into the car. Dick gunned the motor and they sped back to the office. They had seen and heard so many strange things that Dick was beginning to suspect there was more to the case than had first met the eye.

Dick turned off the main road and a few minutes later arrived at Seaview Mansions. He was stepping out of the car when he noticed that Mo's left hand was tightly clenched.

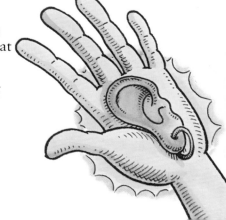

"So, did you find anything inside the Wall of Death?" he asked.

There was a second's pause, then Dick watched as Mo slowly loosened her grip to reveal what she had found.

Back at the Office

M o held out the ear for a closer look but Dick backed away and jumped out of the car. He crashed into a burly man who was hurrying past. Dick mumbled an apology but the man just picked up what he had dropped and walked on without speaking.

Mo helped Dick into the cranky elevator. She hit the fourth-floor button and they clanked jerkily upward. Mo held out the ear again. "It's not real," she said. "I think it must come from a wax figure at the fairground. I found it inside the cashbox belonging to Max, the operator."

"It's a very strange thing to keep in a cashbox," Dick said, idly thinking back to the conversation he had overheard in the Hall of Mirrors. "Max must have thought it was important. I wonder if it's connected with..."

Dick never finished as the elevator suddenly shuddered to an abrupt halt at the fourth floor. Mo pocketed the ear while Dick staggered out of the elevator and unlocked the office door. They both stepped inside.

Mo produced a pen and notebook. "I have a hunch that if we are going to find Dodgem we must investigate everything we've seen and heard so far. The ear, the note with the wax seal, the strange trio, Sharkey..."

"That name rings a bell," Dick interrupted. "I'm sure I saw something on him in the batch of 'S' files I tidied up earlier. Where are they?"

18

Dick had just found the 'S' drawer when there was a knock on the door. "I'll get it," Mo volunteered. She opened the door, just in time to hear footsteps clattering down the stairs below. Then she spotted a brown envelope on the door mat. "I wonder what's in it," Mo muttered.

"Let's find out," Dick replied. As he cleared a space on the top of the desk and began to unfasten the flap of the envelope, his nostrils twitched. There was a faint smell that reminded him of something, of flowers. He shrugged and pulled out the contents.

There is more to the case than you have been told. I found this book of matches by the Wall of Death

A friend

Mo examined the photograph and the matches, then she read the handwritten message. "Very mysterious," she said. "I wonder who this person is in the photo? And who is 'a friend'?"

Dick scratched his head. The case was certainly getting more and more complicated, but they were no closer to finding Dodgem. "What do you think we should do now?" he asked, but before Mo could answer the telephone rang.

"Deckchair Detective Agency. How can we help?" Dick said, picking up the receiver.

Dick heard a woman's voice. Mo moved closer and they listened intently to what the caller said, but before they could speak, she hung up. Would she call back? They had to wait . .

This is a friend. Look at the contents of the envelope. I can't speak now in case the call is traced. I will call back with vital information.

19

The Mystery Caller

The Deckchair Detectives waited inside the office.

Then the phone rang.

Dick grabbed the receiver.

Hello. Who is this?

It is too dangerous to reveal my identity. I delivered the envelope to you.

The mystery caller was speaking from a nearby phone booth.

If you want to find out more about the fairground fires, then listen carefully. I will say this only once.

Meanwhile, inside a darkened room not very far from Seaview Mansions, unfriendly ears were listening in on the mysterious telephone call. As Mo edged closer to the receiver, she and Dick were unaware that a tape recorder was whirring slowly, recording every word. Clearly they were not the only ones interested in the mystery caller...

This matter extends beyond the fairground. The fires are just the tip of a dangerous iceberg. Do you have the photograph I sent you?

Please go on. We're all ears.

Yes, it's on the desk in front of me.

The man in it is Mr. Smith - the watchman for Toucan Warehouse at the downtown docks. He has useful information, but he has vanished. He was last seen heading for an appointment at the Lido de Luxe. Find him and you will discover more.

In the darkened room a shadowy figure hissed to the man with the headphones.

Who is this caller? She knows that we nabbed Mr. Smith.

But how...? Hello... She's hung up again.

No. The trio in the mirrors mentioned a watchman at the docks. Mr. Smith? My instinct tells me there's a connection between his vanishing and Max's disappearance.

What should we do? Do you think it's a hoax?

Let's go to the Lido and ask some questions. Someone may have seen something.

Good idea. And bring those 'S' files along too.

They are going to the Lido. Follow them. You must do something to throw them off our scent.

The Lido de Luxe

Dick drove to the Lido, dodging and weaving through the traffic. The breeze ruffled Mo's hair and cleared her head as she ran through her notes on the facts of the case. "There have been three fires at the fairground and we know that Max, the operator of the Wall of Death is missing. We overheard three villains at the fairground, but we don't know who they are. There's also something going on at the docks, and then there's our mystery caller who told us that someone else – a watchman at the docks – is missing."

"We've got a glove and a cigar butt belonging to Dodgem," Mo continued. "They were both found by Carlotta at the scene of the first two fires. There's also the note with the strange seal and the ear. Then we have a torn book of matches sent by our mystery caller and the photograph of Mr. Smith. What does it all add up to?"

Dick shrugged, regained control of the car and pulled up beside some wrought iron gates. They spotted the Lido through the bushes, but they failed to notice the sinister figure watching their every move...

Dick tried to open the gates, only to find they were locked. "That's no problem, follow me," Mo said, squeezing through the railings. A few tugs, yanks and ouches later, Dick joined her and they crept into the Lido. Mo whistled in amazement as she reached the poolside. She could see why it was called the Lido de Luxe, but now what? There was no one around to answer questions about Mr. Smith, the missing watchman.

"Just keep your eyes peeled for any clues or evidence that might prove Mr. Smith was here," Dick whispered.

Mo checked through the foliage beside the pool and sighed. This was pointless, she didn't even know what she should be looking for. She turned around and spotted a sudden movement by a statue. But before she could focus properly she was distracted by Dick's loud gasp.

Foul Play

Before Mo could move, Dick jumped into the pool. A few tense seconds later his head broke through the surface as he struggled to keep a hold on the heavy, water-logged figure.

"Give me a hand," gasped Dick, swimming to the side. Mo reached down and heaved the body out of the pool.

Gasping for air, Dick clambered out of the water. "Tell me the worst," he said, wiping his eyes. "How bad is he?"

"See for yourself," Mo answered.

Dick slowly looked down. The drowned man was a statue!

"That's where it came from," Mo said, pointing to a damaged pedestal. "And this looks very much like Mr. Smith's hat."

"I'm beginning to suspect foul play," Dick muttered as he dripped his way over to Mo. "All the evidence here points to a struggle in which Mr. Smith's hat was crushed and the statue was knocked off its pedestal."

"If my deduction is correct, that leaves us with one vital question to answer," Dick continued. "Who was Mr. Smith's assailant?"

"What about this?" Mo asked, picking up a black glove. "It's a perfect match with the one Carlotta found. Dodgem seems to be getting very careless."

CRACK. The sound of a twig snapping rang through the night air like a gunshot. Dick dived for cover. "Get up," hissed Mo. "Someone's out there, hiding in the bushes. Let's get them."

Dick went left, Mo headed right. Eyes straining and hearts pounding, they crashed through bushes and ducked under branches, chasing after the shadowy figure ahead.

Mo stopped suddenly. She had lost the figure in the darkness, or had she? Over there! Mo pounced. At that moment Dick spotted someone heading straight for him. "Got you," he yelled launching himself into a tackle. "OUCH."

Mo and Dick staggered unsteadily to their feet. A sudden gust of wind parted the clouds in the evening sky and the park was flooded with moonlight. Mo spotted a dark outline dash out of the bushes and sprint over to the gates.

They set off at top speed, but by the time they reached the entrance the mystery figure had scaled the gates and been swallowed up by the night. Dick and Mo heard a car start, then screech around a distant corner.

"Who was that man, and what was he doing here?" Dick mused. "Now we'll never know. Whoever he was has escaped."

"But he's left part of his jacket on the spikes," Mo replied. "Let's get it down. It might be useful."

Good Luck at Last?

Dick yanked impatiently at the torn jacket. The material held firm for a second then suddenly it was free. Dick knelt down as a stream of objects fell out of a pocket. Mo switched on the car headlights and joined Dick. "Look at all this," Dick exclaimed, as he examined their finds. "I have a feeling our luck is about to change. Something here must help us with the case."

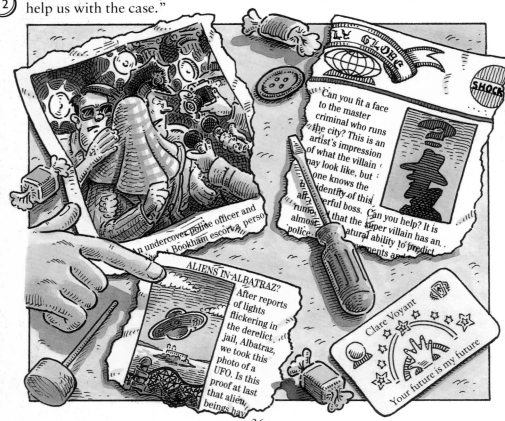

Can you fit a face to the master criminal who runs the city? This is an artist's impression of what the villain may look like, but no one knows the identity of this powerful boss. Can you help? It is rumoured that the super villain has an almost natural ability to predict police movements and

An undercover police officer and secret Bookham escort a person

ALIENS IN ALBATRAZ?
After reports of lights flickering in the derelict jail, Albatraz, we took this photo of a UFO. Is this proof at last that alien beings hav

Clare Voyant
Your future is my future

Dick's brain was racing. He was sure he had seen something or someone in the photo before, but he felt so muddled that he couldn't put the pieces into place. "We need more information," he muttered. "But where can we get it?"

"Search me," answered Mo, then suddenly she remembered something. She reached into the car and unlocked the glove compartment. "These are the 'S' files you told me to bring from the office," she said. "Look! Here's something on Sharkey, and what about the picture on this document? It's identical to the seal on the note we found in the Hall of Mirrors."

"That's brilliant," Dick grinned. "We're getting somewhere at last. Once we've read everything, let's check out the downtown docks."

The Downtown Docks

Dick cut the engine and turned off the headlights. The car rolled to a silent halt in a dark alley beside Toucan Warehouse. Dick peered down at the dashboard clock – it was two minutes to midnight. Staying in the shadows, Mo crept to the corner of the warehouse and stared around.

The loading doors at the front of the building were brightly lit by overhead street lamps. Apart from a scavenging cat, the docks were deserted. All was quiet except for the slapping of water against the sea wall and the chugging of a distant boat out in the bay.

"There doesn't seem to be anybody around," Mo whispered. She stepped back into the shadows and sat down by an overflowing bin. Dick yawned hugely and began flicking a coin.

It was spinning in mid air when Dick heard a match striking. Light flared up at a window in the warehouse opposite. The flickering flame illuminated an instantly recognizable silhouette – Dodgem!

Dick gasped. The coin hit the floor with a clank. Dick grabbed Mo's shoulder and pointed her to the window, but Dodgem was gone. Dick rubbed his eyes. It had happened so quickly, maybe he had been dreaming? There was only one way to find out.

Dick and Mo sped across to the warehouse and flattened themselves against one of the locked doors. Mo pressed her ear against the thick wood. She could just make out the dull murmur of heavy machinery. "We must get in and find out what Dodgem's up to," hissed Dick. "But how?"

Mo spotted a way up to the first floor. "Don't make a sound," she hissed. "I'm going in."

Dick watched as Mo clambered up some crates, swung onto an open loading door and knelt on a narrow window ledge. "Come on," she whispered. "It's your turn, I'll give you a hand." Dick gulped then shinned up a drainpipe and joined Mo on the ledge. They slipped silently through the open door, crept along a dusty corridor to a balcony and peered down. There was no sign of Dodgem, but the characters below looked vaguely familiar. Dick wracked his brains, but he couldn't figure out where he had seen them before.

14

Inside the Warehouse

What were they doing down there? Dick and Mo had to get a closer look, but how? They were bound to be spotted. They needed a diversion.

Outside, a ship's whistle blew twice. Right on cue the machinery was turned off, then two men opened the doors and began picking up the crates. Dick and Mo crept quietly downstairs. Now they could discover what was going on and find out what was in the crates.

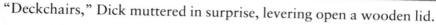

"Deckchairs," Dick muttered in surprise, levering open a wooden lid.

"Money," gasped Mo, as she thrust her hand deeper into the crate and pulled out the top layer under the straw packaging. The gang members were forgers! "So that's what the dockside operation is all about," Mo said grabbing a wad of the counterfeit money. "I'll just take this as evidence."

"We must search the warehouse thoroughly," Mo continued. "We've got to find Dodgem again." Dick nodded eagerly and they crept past a small office. Suddenly they heard the screech of brakes outside, followed by loud shouts and the pounding of feet. Dick and Mo hit the deck as a burst of gunfire sent bullets whizzing over their heads.

Dick's heart pounded as he waited for the order, "Come out with your hands up." But it never came. Instead he and Mo heard crashes, bangs and angry yells. Cautiously they peered out from their hiding place.

The docks were in chaos. The counterfeiters were being attacked by a bunch of gangsters wearing sharp suits and hats. Mo recognized the leader of the second group – holding a megaphone and shouting instructions to his men was Sharkey. The realization of what was happening suddenly struck her. "We're in the middle of a gang war," she breathed in disbelief. "This is amazing."

"This is a disaster," Dick said, tugging at her shoulder. "Let's get out of here while we're still in one piece."

Getaway

As stray bullets ricocheted around their ears, Mo agreed it was time to go. She had taken two paces when Dick gasped. Mo turned to see him frantically dabbing at red stains on his shirt.

"I... I'm hit," Dick quavered. "Go on without me." But Mo just smiled and pointed to a bullet-ridden can of red paint dripping from the shelf above.

Gingerly, Dick checked himself for bullet holes then followed Mo in her search for an escape route. While the rival gangs were still battling each other on the waterfront, Mo spotted a side door. She tried the handle. With a sigh of relief she discovered it was unlocked.

Mo pushed the door open and peered out. Their car was parked a few feet away. She stared around, the coast was clear. Dick and Mo dashed across the alley and dived into the car. Dick fumbled for his keys.

"Please start," Dick begged. "Please."

The engine choked, spluttered and died. Dick groaned loudly. Behind them came an angry yell. They had been spotted!

Dick desperately turned the key again. Pistol shots rang out from behind them. Suddenly the windscreen shattered and cracked. "Get down," Dick hissed. "Here we go – this is our last chance."

VROOOOM. The engine roared into life at last. Dick stepped on the accelerator. The wheels screeched and the car shot off down the narrow alley. Up ahead was a brick wall! Dick yanked on the brake and they took the left-hand turn on two wheels. Mo opened her eyes as they bounced back onto solid ground. They were still alive, and Toucan Warehouse was receding into the distance.

Dick checked his rearview mirror. No one was on their tail. He eased off the gas, took a left turn and headed back into town. "So now we know what Dodgem is mixed up with," he began. "I bet Mr. Smith disappeared because he stumbled on the counterfeiting racket."

"I agree," Mo answered. "But I've been racking my brains and there's still one thing I don't understand. What's the connection between Dodgem and the fairground fires?"

Dick groaned, he didn't know either. They were still miles away from wrapping up the case. As Dick tried to see a way through the muddle of confusing evidence, a car pulled up at the lights beside them. Dick sniffed the air and wrinkled up his nose at the bitter smell of cigar smoke. He glanced across and gasped as he recognized the driver – it was Dodgem!

"Stay on his tail," Mo hissed. The lights changed. Dodgem accelerated ahead and Dick followed. Then, Dodgem turned off the main road and bumped down dusty side tracks. The miles sped by and the sun beat down. "This is easy," Dick thought. "Dodgem obviously hasn't spotted..."

Dick never finished. Up ahead Dodgem accelerated quickly. As Dick changed into overdrive a blue car screamed past. Mo saw a hand reach out of the car and drop rusty nails on the road ahead. "Look out," she shouted, but it was too late.

Dick slammed on the brakes and wrestled with the wheel as they screeched to a punctured halt. Dick and Mo could only watch as Dodgem and the other car sped off in a cloud of dust.

The Desert Garage

The dejected duo slowly climbed out of the car to inspect the damage. The groan of cooling metal and the hiss of escaping air was accompanied by Dick sighing. The car was beyond repair. There was only one thing to do – walk for help. But which way? There was no traffic or any other sign of life in either direction.

"We may as well head in the same direction as Dodgem," Mo said.

Dick trudged along after Mo. The blistering sun blazed down on them and clouds of dust scratched at their throats, making them cough and choke. Dick and Mo toiled on, occasionally stopping to rest in the shade of a prickly roadside cactus. Dick fanned his face as a blast of hot air burned into his lungs. "Let's stop," he croaked, licking his cracked lips. "We're not getting anywhere like this."

A snake slithered out of the way as Dick sat down by the side of the road. Mo stared hard into the heat haze ahead and spotted something shimmering in the distance... Was it a mirage? No, it was a garage.

Dick caught up with Mo a few paces later. "I hope it's not deserted," said Mo, scanning the peeling paintwork on the ramshackle building. "It's not exactly the busiest road in the world."

"Hello," Dick shouted, racing ahead. "Anyone there?"

Nothing disturbed the silence except for a lizard scurrying up a wooden post and the squeak of a door swinging on rusty hinges. Then, as they walked closer, they heard faint voices coming from behind a dusty window. Dick froze as he recognized one of the voices and tried to make out what they were saying, but Mo wasn't paying attention.

"We're in luck," Mo said, and before Dick could stop her, she rapped on the glass. The sound of voices stopped abruptly then a figure appeared in the doorway. It was Tom, the fairground security guard! What was he doing here?

"Not you two again," Tom groaned as he recognized Dick and Mo. "Come here," he snapped impatiently. "We've got some serious talking to do."

"No way," shouted Dick, grabbing Mo's arm and pulling her out of Tom's reach. "Run for it."

Dick and Mo sprinted past heaps of rusting car parts. Mo looked over her shoulder and gasped, Tom was close behind them and getting closer. Just then he launched himself into a flying tackle. Quick as a flash, Mo swung an old car seat around to block him. To her amazement, Tom landed on a spring and went flying...

Vital Evidence

Mo checked to see if Tom was all right. He was out for the count and snoring loudly. That left the other person Tom had been talking to, whoever that might be.

Just then an engine roared. Dick spun around and saw a familiar car speeding down the road. He recognized the driver at once. Dodgem was getting away. Dick aimed a sharp stone at the car's back wheel. It missed and bounced harmlessly into a ditch.

Dick hurried back to the garage. Tom was still sleeping peacefully, but where was Mo? A shout from a doorway led Dick into a small untidy room. Mo looked up from a pile of papers and photos on a table top.

"This is Dodgem's hideout," she said excitedly. "Tom must be his accomplice at the fairground. Things are falling into place now. Look at the wax seals on the messages – it's the Scarab Society again, and this is the plate which they use to forge money. These photos look like pictures of their criminal activities. I wonder why they took them?"

19

Max is getting dangerous. He's found our secret in the Dragon Temple and wants to talk. A torch job should do the trick. I shall personally take great pleasure in supplying the match, then we shall take him to our secret headquarters. Mr Smith has also been snooping around too much. He must be dealt with. Arrange a rendezvous trap and then take him to join Max for a long island holiday.

URGENT I have just received a tip-off from an informer. Our dockside operation is no longer safe from Sharkey. One final batch of money must be made up tonight, then use the boat to transfer everything to our secret headquarters.

Mo's question wasn't the only nagging doubt in Dick's mind. It looked as if Dodgem was the leader of the Scarab Society, but as he examined the evidence, Dick felt he was missing something.

"Let's contact Carlotta," Mo continued. "Here's her number." A distant alarm sounded in Dick's head when he saw the scrap of paper Mo was holding, but he didn't know why. In the meantime, Mo phoned Carlotta and told her what they had discovered.

The fairground owner seemed pleased with the news. Mo listened to Carlotta's suggestion and had just agreed to meet her when CLICK, the line went dead. What was going on? Dick spotted Tom lurching their way, wire cutters in hand. Dick gulped and turned white while Mo stuffed the evidence in a green folder. She grabbed Dick and they both dived out of the back window.

Mo picked herself up from the dust and stared around frantically. "This way," she shouted, heading for Tom's car. She yanked open the door and reached for the ignition... there were no keys. What should they do now? Mo moved out of the way as Dick crouched low beneath the steering wheel and fumbled with the casing. Seconds later, the engine coughed then spluttered to life.

Dick spun the wheel. The car swerved around Tom, hit a fuel pump, then bounced and jolted on-to the road. As they headed back into town, Mo turned to watch Tom become a smaller and smaller dot on the horizon.

"Where did you learn that trick?" Mo asked in amazement.

"From a villain called Hotwire Harry," Dick replied sheepishly. "I had a hunch that it might come in useful one day."

Fairground Fun

Dick and Mo arrived at the moonlit fairground just after five o'clock in the morning. Dick was feeling apprehensive. He wasn't sure why, but vague worries had been lurking at the back of his mind ever since they had discovered Dodgem's hideout. Perhaps they should be looking at this case from another angle . . .

"Come on," Mo hissed, pushing Dick through the turnstile and following him into the fair. Silver moonlight threw sharp, stabbing shadows onto the ground and made the roller coaster look like a huge iron skeleton. "This is spooky," whispered Dick as they made their way past the helter-skelter.

Just then, neon lights around them began to hum and buzz. Mo's face turned pink while Dick took on a greenish hue. "H . . . hello, who . . . who's there?" stammered Dick. "Is that you Carlotta?"

Hand over the evidence.

Do as we say.

Then no one will get hurt.

Three figures stepped out of the shadows and hissed out orders. Mo instantly recognized the villains' faces from the warehouse. With a sickening lurch in his stomach, Dick realized he had heard their voices before. The villains were the strange trio from the Hall of Mirrors. A question flashed through his mind. How did these villains know that Dick and Mo would be at the fairground tonight? But the only thought in Mo's head was escape. She had already spotted a way out. She grabbed Dick and they ripped through a coconut shy. Dick snatched at some coconuts and wrenched one free from its pole.

As Dick dashed after Mo something whistled past his shoulder. They turned around as knives cut through the air and sliced into the wooden boarding behind, quivering where they landed. Liquid trickled over Dick's hand. "I knew that coconut would come in handy," he thought.

Dick and Mo ran for their lives, jumping over ropes, dodging past the bumper cars and weaving through the waltzers, until they reached the exit. But it was guarded by one of the trio holding a lighted torch.

The villain lifted a bottle to his lips. Mo could smell fuel. Suddenly she realized what was about to happen. "DUCK," she yelled.

They dived for cover as a tongue of bright orange flame whooshed up to them, spitting angrily and scorching everything in its path.

Apart from singed eyebrows, Mo and Dick were unhurt. Before the human flame thrower could reload, they were back on their feet. They sprinted past the Big Dipper and headed for the roller coaster.

"Get into one of the cars," Dick ordered. He hit the 'on' switch and jumped in beside her. The car rocketed along the rails, taking Mo's breath away.

Behind them the two villains were about to follow but they stared along the track and changed their minds. Dick glanced ahead. Horror-struck, he knew what the third villain had been doing . . .

The track's been sabotaged.

Crash Landing

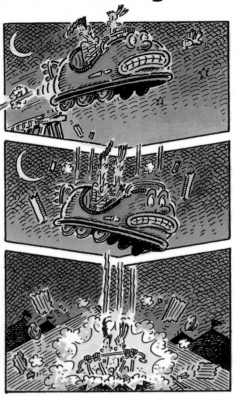

Dick's desperate shout hung in the air as the car hit the broken track and flew off into the night. Mo's life flashed quickly before her eyes while Dick's cry choked off into a strangled scream.

They raced up through the night sky and for a few seconds all was quiet apart from the wind whistling through their hair. The car hovered for a moment and then began plummeting to the ground. Dick stared through his fingers in horror – they were heading for one of the shows.

CRASH. Splinters flew and glass shattered as the car smashed through the roof of the fairground show. It bounced once before collapsing into pieces. Mo and Dick felt every bone in their body shudder, then blackness descended.

The dust began to settle on Dick and Mo, who were out cold. As they lay dazed among the rubble, they were unaware that the three villains were heading to where the car had crash-landed. Meanwhile, above Dick and Mo's heads, a sliver of wood swayed from a shattered rafter. It broke free and clattered to the floor.

"What's going on?" Dick groaned. "Ouch!" Brightly tinted stars spun around his head but they soon disappeared as he remembered the knives, the flame and then the crash. He was all right, what about Mo? "Are you OK?" he hissed.

"I'll be fine," Mo answered groggily. "Just tell me what hit us and where we are."

Dick staggered unsteadily to his feet and stared around. He blinked twice and waited for his sight to return to normal. He rubbed his eyes again, but the strange figures and Chinese decorations wouldn't go away. Then it dawned on him – this was the Dragon Temple.

Mo gasped. In a flash she remembered that the Dragon Temple was mentioned in one of the notes with the scarab seal, but before she could tell Dick, she caught the sound of a door opening, followed by heavy footsteps. "We've got visitors," she said. "And I don't think they've come to ask about our health. Let's get out of here."

Mo grabbed Dick's arm, but he wouldn't move. He was staring at one of the wax figures. Mo suddenly realized why . . . the guard's right ear was missing. Mo fumbled in her pockets and held up the ear she had found in the Wall of Death – it was a perfect match.

Into the Dragon's Mouth

M o spotted a red button sticking out of the side of the wax figure's head. The broken ear fitted perfectly into position. "Stand back," Mo whispered, pressing hard on the button. There was a loud click, followed by the sound of cogwheels grinding. Dick jumped as the dragon's jaw sprang open with a loud clang. He peered into the open mouth, and could just see a flight of steps leading down into a dark tunnel.

Mo heard sounds of the three villains behind. "Let's go," she said, pushing Dick into the tunnel. As they stumbled down the steps, the entrance snapped shut behind them. There was no going back now.

Dick took the green folder and put it in his pocket as Mo dug out a box of matches. By the light of the flickering flame they crept cautiously forwards.

"I guess this is an old smuggler's tunnel," whispered Dick. "But where does it lead?"

They didn't have to wait too long to find out. Ten matches later the tunnel ended at a solid wall of stone. Mo spotted footholds, cut into the rock, leading up to a small wooden trap door.

23

Dick looked on as Mo planted her feet securely in the footholds and pushed against the trap door with all her strength. It opened a few reluctant inches, letting shafts of light pierce the gloom below. Mo paused for a second. Where would they come out?

Mo lifted the trapdoor higher and looked around. They were in some sort of courtyard. Half-ruined watch towers jutted up into the sky while coils of rusting wire sprawled over the grass. This was Albatraz, the abandoned city jail. The tunnel had led Dick and Mo under the sea and out onto the island prison.

"At least we know why Max disappeared," hissed Dick, crawling out beside Mo. "It all ties in with that typed note we found in Dodgem's hideout and what the trio said in the Hall of Mirrors. Max must have stumbled on the tunnel entrance. He took the ear as evidence, but the Scarab Society got wind of him and torched his ride."

"You're right, but why is the tunnel such a big secret?" Mo tried one of the steel doors that led from the courtyard into the main building – it was unlocked. The door swung open silently and Dick and Mo peered into a deserted hall. Then they spotted the two prisoners and the scarab flags. This had to be the Scarab Society headquarters.

Prisoners

Dick and Mo dashed over to the surprised prisoners. Dick recognized Mr. Smith instantly. The other man had to be Max, "Don't worry," he said, "We're friends. We're going to get you out of here." As he grabbed a large bunch of keys from the table, Mr. Smith and Max began talking...

I told a friend of mine about the forgers. She said her father would help me, but I was captured before I could meet him.

I found the tunnel and planned to hand over the ear to David, my ex-boss. Since he was forced to sell out a year ago he's been investigating the goings-on at the fair and has collected evidence.

24

Their stories set Dick's brain racing. At last he was sure he was close to solving the case. If only he could have some time to think it all through logically, and find the right key to unlock the cell.

Meanwhile Mo was investigating the hall. She delved into some familiar packing cases and pulled out bundles of cash. "More forgeries I bet," Mo muttered, examining one carefully in the light. A sudden movement outside caught her eye. The three fairground villains were emerging from the trapdoor in the courtyard. "Here comes trouble," she yelled, dashing over to another window. She stared out and gasped. Dodgem and Tom were landing on one side of the island. From another window she spotted Sharkey and his mob.

"We've got to hide," Mo shouted. She spotted a rickety staircase leading up to a balcony. "Follow me Dick, and pick up those knives from the floor. I've got a plan."

All was quiet in the hall until suddenly one of the doors burst open and the fairground villains raced in. They froze as the door opposite was thrown open – in dashed Dodgem and Tom. Seconds later Sharkey and his gang appeared. The villains stared at each other in amazement.

"Now," Mo shouted. Before anyone below could move, she and Dick cut through the nets hanging from the balcony. The floor below was filled with struggling figures. Dick raced downstairs to check their catch.

He was in midstep when his nostrils suddenly twitched at the familiar smell of violets. Dick spotted Clare Voyant striding into the hall. Her earrings caught Dick's eye, triggering a distant memory in his mind.

25

Just then Dick missed the bottom step and landed with a bump. His head swam and so did his thoughts. Dick looked up and saw Carlotta standing over him. In a flash everything became clear. "I'm so glad you're safe," Carlotta breathed. "You've done a marvellous job."

"Correct," Dick replied, jumping to his feet. "Now I will explain the case of the fairground fires, and what's more I shall reveal the identity of the Scarab Society boss."

DON'T TURN THE PAGE YET. You now have all the information you need to solve the case of the fairground fires. Can you reveal the identity of the leader of the Scarab Society?

26

Dick Reveals All

Mo ran down to join Dick as he began. "At first, the case of the fairground fires appeared simple. The evidence against Dodgem seemed conclusive, but when Mo found Dodgem's glove at the Lido, it began to seem too neat. Would Dodgem really be so careless as to drop all those clues?"

"I didn't know what to make of it. But when I overheard Dodgem telling Tom that he had taken the plates to stop the forging operation, I began to wonder if Dodgem might be innocent. The proof was supplied by Max. The photos and the notes at Dodgem's hideout were not evidence against Dodgem, but were the evidence Dodgem had collected in his investigation of the fair. Max trusted Dodgem and was going to tell him about the tunnel, which is why he was kidnapped."

"But if Dodgem was innocent, who was framing him and why?" continued Dick. "The Scarab Society knew that Dodgem was on their trail, but thanks to Sharkey and his gang, they were so busy that they couldn't find him. That's where we came in. Dodgem was set up to look like a crook, then we were supposed to find Dodgem and lead the real villains to him. That's why we were hired by the leader of the Scarab Society . . . that's why we were hired by Carlotta Bottle!"

"This detective work has gone to your head," Carlotta said, smiling. "It's an interesting theory, but you have no proof."

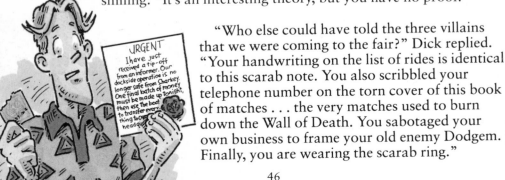

"Who else could have told the three villains that we were coming to the fair?" Dick replied. "Your handwriting on the list of rides is identical to this scarab note. You also scribbled your telephone number on the torn cover of this book of matches . . . the very matches used to burn down the Wall of Death. You sabotaged your own business to frame your old enemy Dodgem. Finally, you are wearing the scarab ring."

"You think you're so clever," Carlotta snarled. "But you forgot one thing – my bodyguard. He bugged your phone and planted Dodgem's glove at the Lido. And he's right behind you. Hands up!"

Dick and Mo glumly did as they were ordered. Was this it? Was all their detective work going to end like this? As Carlotta's henchman stepped up to them, Mo spotted a flash of purple. An instant later, a crystal ball flew through the air, right on target.

The burly bodyguard collapsed to the floor. Carlotta grabbed for his gun, but Mo kicked it away. The pistol spun towards the net where a large, tattooed hand reached out and engulfed it. Mo remembered seeing the tattoo before, in a photo dropped by Carlotta's bodyguard. Now she recognized Tom as the undercover policeman in that photo.

Carlotta dashed for the door, just as police burst into the room. They handcuffed Carlotta and surrounded the net. Dodgem and Tom crawled out. "Well done, you two," Tom said to Dick and Mo. "We've wanted to nail this gang for ages. Thanks to you, the case is all wrapped up."

The villains were led away, but one thing was troubling Mo. Where did Clare Voyant fit in? "I worked out that you were our mystery caller from the scent of violets on the envelope you delivered," Dick said. "But I only realized your true identity when I recognized your earrings."

Mo gasped as Clare Voyant took off her hat and a wig to reveal . . . Viola Dodgem. After she explained her story, Dick turned to Mo. "All our hard work deserves a break. What do you say?"

"You must be joking," replied Mo. "Let's get back to the office. There may be another case for the Deckchair Detectives . . ."

I disguised myself to get a job at the fair and prove my father's innocence.

Detective Guide

This page will give you some help in solving the case. The numbers written here refer to the numbers inside the magnifying glasses found throughout the book.

1 There may be some useful information in the newspaper.
2 Take a good look at the evidence – it may come in handy.
3 Why is the security guard evesdropping outside the door?
4 What's suspicious about the whispering voice? It mentions Max, maybe it will make more sense later.
5 Look and listen carefully.
6 The message may not mean much now, but follow Dick's hunch and save it for later.
7 Flowers?
8 What are matches used for?
9 You're one step ahead of Dick and Mo here. Keep your eyes open.
10 Do you recognize the sinister stranger?
11 A perfect match?
12 Some of the information might be useful.
13 Read the documents carefully. They may contain useful information.
14 Have you seen any of these people before?
15 The symbol on the crates looks familiar.
16 Dick and Mo haven't got time to search the warehouse properly, but you should keep your eyes peeled.
17 Does this hand look familiar?
18 This conversation may be worth remembering.
19 Is Mo jumping to conclusions? Think back to the conversation which Dick overhead outside the deserted garage.
20 Dick may be right.
21 Does that ripped piece of paper match up with something you've seen before?
22 The villains seem to be expecting Dick and Mo.
23 Remember the voices Mo and Dick overheard outside the Hall of Mirrors.
24 Who is David?
25 Flowery smells again! Have you seen those earrings before?
26 A handy hint is just what you need here.

Did You Spot?

Now you've read the story and solved the mystery, check whether you spotted every clue. If you have any difficulty reading this try holding this page in front of a mirror.

Carlotta was wearing the scarab ring from the very beginning.

The purple shadow glimpsed by Dick beside the Wall of Death on page 15 was none other than Clare Voyant, alias Viola Dodgem. This was where she discovered Carlotta's torn match book.

Wherever she went, whether in disguise or not, Viola Dodgem always wore a flowery perfume smelling of violets. Viola means 'violet' in Latin.

Dick backed into Carlotta's henchman on page 18 as he was leaving Seaview Mansions. He was holding a screwdriver – probably used to bug the Deckchair Detectives' telephone.

Carlotta's henchman looked a bit like Dodgem – a red herring that may have confused you.

In the darkened room, not so far from Seaview Mansions (pages 20-21), the mystery speaker is wearing a scarab ring – is Carlotta.

At the Lido, Carlotta's henchman dropped a glove ... a false clue to convince Dick and Mo that Dodgem had somehow nabbed Mr Smith. It's a pity he dropped another left-handed glove as the one on page 12 was also left-handed – Carlotta has made a mistake. The statue was also the work of Carlotta's henchman. In fact, Mr Smith was taken by Carlotta's three fairground villains.

The contents of the henchman's pockets were useful, but there were also a lot of red herrings. The screwdriver on page 26 was the one used by Carlotta's henchman to bug the Deckchair office. The Aliens in Albaraz is nonsense although the flickering lights were evidence of the Scarab Society's activities there. The newspaper article showing the crime leader's silhouette was way off mark. The henchman had Clare Voyant's card – perhaps she had recently read his palm.

The Scarab Society probably used the fairground tunnel from Albaraz in their notorious breakout from the Albaraz jail (as mentioned in the Deckchair Document on page 26).

Did you notice Steve Same (see document on page 27) in the picture on page 29?

If you wondered what Dodgem was doing at the warehouse, he was gathering vital evidence against the Scarab Society's activities. You can see him taking the forging plate on page 30.

Tom is an undercover police officer. You can see the tattoo on his right hand on the photo on page 26.

Viola knew about the Scarab Society's activities from her father. She was the mystery caller on page 19. Viola hoped Dick and Mo would help but couldn't afford to blow her cover at this point.

First published in 1992 by Usborne Publishing Ltd, Usborne House, 83-85 Saffron Hill, London EC1N 8RT, England.
Copyright © 1992 Usborne Publishing Ltd.

The name Usborne and the device 🍥 are Trade Marks of Usborne Publishing Ltd.

First published in America March 1993
Printed in the UK.   UE